Highlights Puzzle Readers

LEVEL 2

Kit and Kaboodle
RIDE A ROLLER COASTER

By Michelle Portice
Art by Mitch Mortimer

HIGHLIGHTS PRESS
Honesdale, Pennsylvania

Stories + Puzzles = Reading Success!

Dear Parents,

Highlights Puzzle Readers are an innovative approach to learning to read that combines puzzles and stories to build motivated, confident readers.

Developed in collaboration with reading experts, the stories and puzzles are seamlessly integrated so that readers are encouraged to read the story, solve the puzzles, and then read the story again. This helps increase vocabulary and reading fluency and creates a satisfying reading experience for any kind of learner. In addition, solving Hidden Pictures puzzles fosters important reading and learning skills such as:

- shape and letter recognition
- letter-sound relationships
- visual discrimination
- logic
- flexible thinking
- sequencing

With high-interest stories, humorous characters, and trademark puzzles, Highlights Puzzle Readers offer a winning combination for inspiring young learners to love reading.

This is Kit.

This is Kaboodle.

They love to **travel**. You can help them on each **adventure**.

As you read the story, find the objects in each **Hidden Pictures** puzzle.

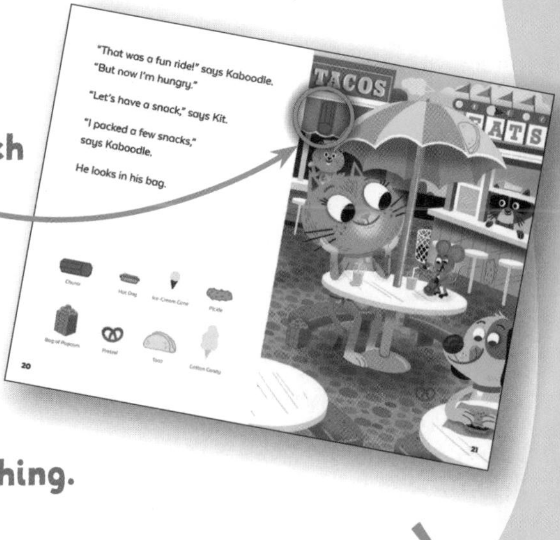

"That was a fun ride!" says Kaboodle. "But now I'm hungry."

"Let's have a snack," says Kit.

"I packed a few snacks," says Kaboodle.

He looks in his bag.

Then check the **Packing List** on pages 30–31 to make sure you found everything.

Happy reading!

WONDER
PARK
TRAM
STOP
W
WONDER
PARK

Kit and Kaboodle are going to Wonder Park. They are ready for an exciting day!

“Wonder Park has the fastest roller coaster,” says Kit.

“It’s also the tallest roller coaster,” says Kaboodle.

“We’re here!” says Kit.

“Not yet,” says Kaboodle.

Kit and Kaboodle ride a tram.

“We’re here!” says Kit.

“Not yet,” says Kaboodle.

They go through the gate.

“We’re here!” says Kit.

“Yes, we’re here!” says Kaboodle.

"Let's play a game," says Kaboodle. "That game looks fun."

"We need to buy tickets to play," says Kit.

"I packed some money we can use to buy tickets," says Kaboodle.

He looks in his bag.

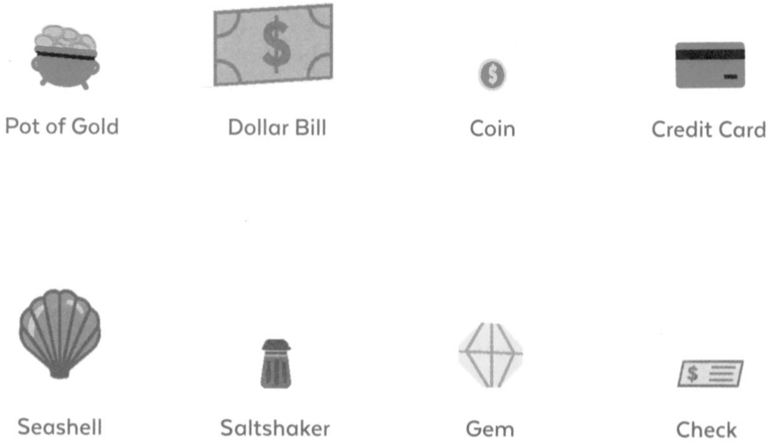

ARTS
KNO K 'EM OVER!!
TICKETS
W

"What a fun prize!" says Kit.
"I hope it will fit in my pack."

"What a fun prize!" says Kaboodle.
"I hope it will fit in my bag."

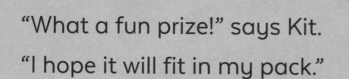

“Should we ride the roller coaster next?” asks Kit.

“Not yet,” says Kaboodle. “What time is the parade?”

“The parade is starting now!” says Kit.

“I packed a few things
we can use to cheer,” says Kaboodle.

He looks in his bag.

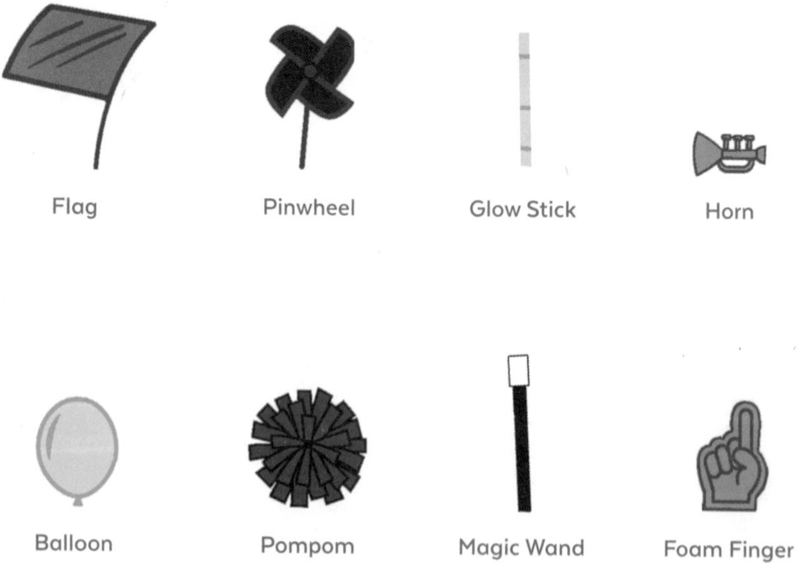

TASTY TREATS
DRINKS!

“What a fun parade!” says Kaboodle.

“Should we ride the roller coaster next?” asks Kit.

“I’m not sure,” says Kaboodle.
“It’s very fast. Let’s ride that ride.”

The ride goes slowly up, up, up.

Then the ride goes down very fast.

SPLASH!

“What a fun ride!” says Kaboodle.
“But now we’re all wet.”

“What are we going to do?” asks Kit.

“I packed a few things
we can use to dry off,” says Kaboodle.

He looks in his bag.

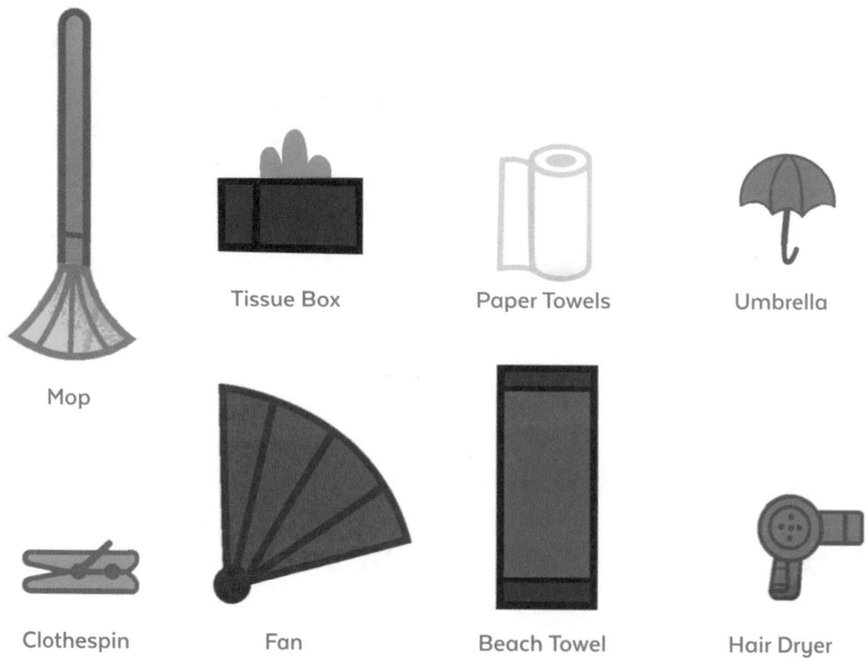

ER'S

"Should we ride the roller coaster next?" asks Kit.

"I'm not sure," says Kaboodle. "It's very tall."

"Let's ride this ride next," says Kit.

The ride goes up, up, up very high.

“Look at the view!” says Kaboodle.

The ride goes down, down, down.

"That was a fun ride!" says Kaboodle.
"But now I'm hungry."

"Let's have a snack," says Kit.

"I packed a few snacks,"
says Kaboodle.

He looks in his bag.

Churro

Hot Dog

Ice-Cream Cone

Pickle

Bag of Popcorn

Pretzel

Taco

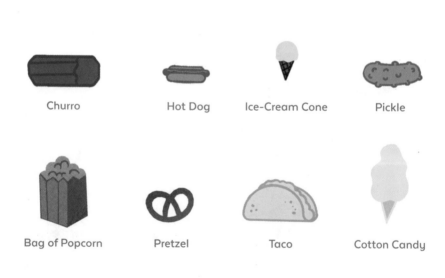

Cotton Candy

ACOS
EATS

Kit and Kaboodle swing on tall swings.

"*Whee!*" says Kit.

They slide down long slides.

"*Whee!*" says Kaboodle.

They bump in fast bumper cars.

"*Whee!*" says Kit.

"*Whee!*" says Kaboodle.

"Those rides were so much fun!" says Kit. "Should we ride the roller coaster?"

"Yes!" says Kaboodle. "I'm ready to ride the roller coaster."

"I'm ready, too," says Kit.

"I packed a few things we can do while we wait in line," says Kaboodle.

He looks in his bag.

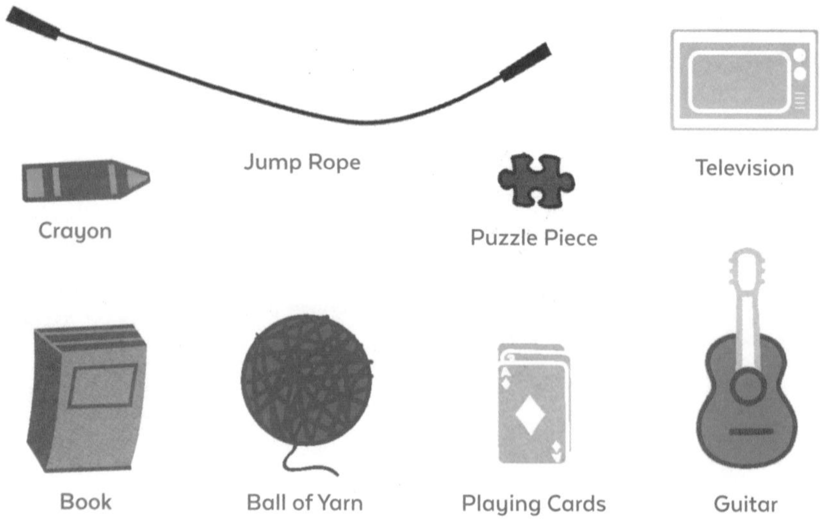

"It's our turn," says Kaboodle.

"Hooray!" says Kit.

The ride goes slowly up, up, up very high.

Then the ride goes down very fast.

"*Whee!*" says Kit.

"*Whee!*" says Kaboodle.

"We did it," says Kaboodle.
"We rode the roller coaster!"

"It was very tall and very fast," says Kit.

"And it was very fun!" says Kaboodle.

"We make a good team," says Kit.

"Where should we go on our next trip?"
asks Kaboodle.

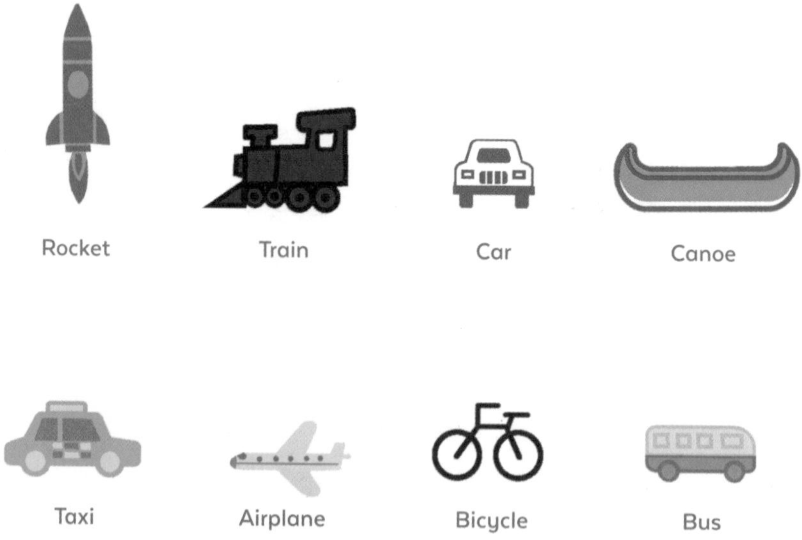

WONDER
PARK
TICKETS
25¢
WIN
EXIT
GO TO SPACE!
TRAVEL BY AIR!

Did you find all the things Kit and

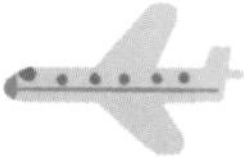
Airplane

Bag of Popcorn

Ball of Yarn

Balloon

Canoe

Car

Check

Churro

Credit Card

Dollar Bill

Fan

Flag

Hair Dryer

Horn

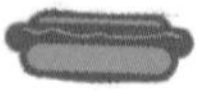
Hot Dog

Ice-Cream Cone

Pickle

Pinwheel

Playing Cards

Pompom

Saltshaker

Seashell

Taco

Taxi

Kaboodle packed for their trip?

Beach Towel

Bicycle

Book

Bus

Clothespin

Coin

Cotton Candy

Crayon

Foam Finger

Gem

Glow Stick

Guitar

Jump Rope

Magic Wand

Mop

Paper Towels

Pot of Gold

Pretzel

Puzzle Piece

Rocket

Television

Tissue Box

Train

Umbrella

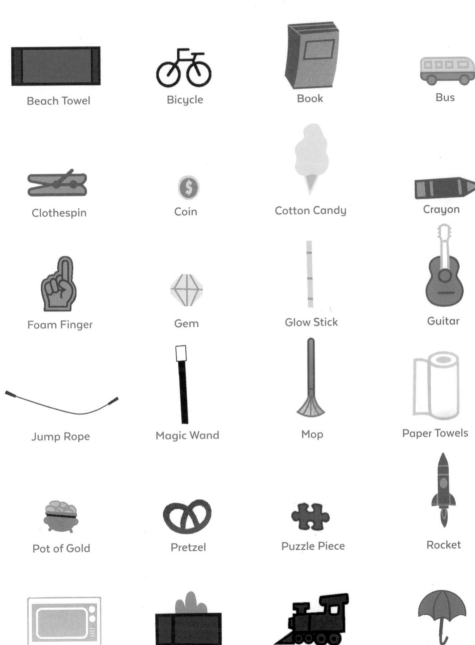

Published by Highlights Press
815 Church Street
Honesdale, Pennsylvania 18431
ISBN (paperback): 978-1-64472-131-5
ISBN (hardcover): 978-1-64472-132-2
ISBN (ebook): 978-1-64472-240-4

Library of Congress Control Number: 2020949605
Manufactured in Melrose Park, IL, USA
Mfg. 03/2021

First edition
Visit our website at Highlights.com.
10 9 8 7 6 5 4 3 2 1

This book has been officially leveled with both the F&P Text Level Gradient™ Leveling System and the Lexile® Text Measure.

For assistance in the preparation of this book, the editors would like to thank Vanessa Maldonado, MSEd, MS Literacy Ed. K–12, Reading/LA Consultant Cert., K–5 Literacy Instructional Coach; and Gina Shaw.